A Lullaby of Love for

Julia

By Suzanne Marshall

A Lullaby of Love
for Julia

Personalized Book for Kids & Bedtime Story
for Baby, Toddler, Children, Boy & Girl
with Gratitude Rhymes & a Cute Cat

Suzanne Marshall

This book is dedicated to

JULIA

who is loved very much!

Julia,

are you ready to give thanks tonight

for all that's peaceful, warm and bright?

Julia,

as the Deer plays guitar with glee,
let's give thanks for you and me
and time together in harmony.

I AM
THANKFUL

Julia,

as the Hippo plays the violin,
let's give thanks for giggles and grins
and belly laughs from deep within.

Julia,

as the Owl drums like a pro,

let's give thanks for all

adventures that help us grow,

even "oopsy-daisies"

and "uh-ohs."

Julia,

as the Giraffe softly sings,

let's give thanks for everything,

like smooches from pooches

and butterfly wings.

Julia,

as the Eagle plays the harp,
let's give thanks for your big heart.
You are brave and you are smart.

Julia,

as the Badger plays the clarinet,

let's give thanks for every breath

that calms us down and helps us rest.

Julia,

as the Antelope plays maracas,

let's give thanks

for cuddles and hugs

and all that's cozy,

comfy and snug.

Julia,

as the Elk plays the cello,

let's give thanks for feeling mellow,

like a spongy, sweet marshmallow.

Julia,

as the Bunny

plays the violin,

let's give thanks

for family and friends,

and love that never,

ever ends.

Julia,

as the Fox plays the flute,

I give thanks that you are YOU.

You are loved and loving too.

Julia,

as the Bear plays the sax,

as you sleep, as you relax,

I LOVE YOU

to the moon and back.

GOODNIGHT JULIA

(Pictured above: Suzanne Marshall and Abby Underdog)

About the Author

Suzanne Marshall writes to inspire, engage and empower children. Her books are full of affirmations, inspiration and unconditional love. An honors graduate of Smith College, Suzanne has made it her misson to spread love through storytelling. Learn more at **LiveWellMedia.com**.

Credits

All illustrations have been edited by the author. Musical animals and hot-air balloon: © ddraw (freepik). Main cat, cat friend & sleeping kitty: © dazdraperma (fotosearch). Puppy: yayayoyo (fotosearch). Moon and lantern: © zzve (fotosearch). Floral ladder: © colematt (fotosearch). Additional elements were curated from freepik.

Made with love by
LiveWellMedia.com

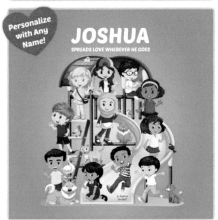

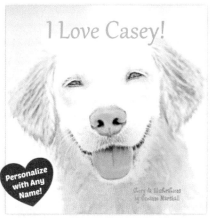

Made in the USA
Monee, IL
11 December 2023

48885044R00024